Sleeping Beauty

Alexis Roumanis

FICTION READALONG
AV²
BY WEIGL
ADDED VALUE · AUDIO VISUAL

www.av2books.com

Your AV² Media Enhanced book gives you a fiction readalong online. Log on to www.av2books.com and enter the unique book code from this page to use your readalong.

AV² Readalong Navigation

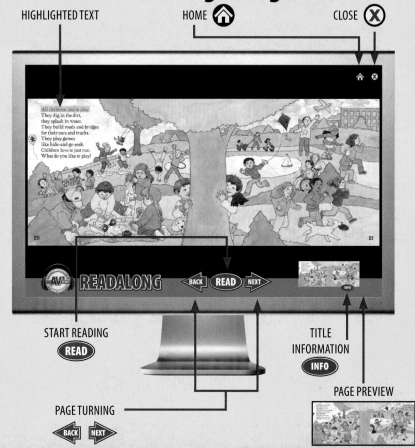

Go to **www.av2books.com**, and enter this book's unique code.

BOOK CODE

K 6 8 3 9 5 9

AV² by Weigl brings you media enhanced books that support active learning.

HIGHLIGHTED TEXT　　HOME　　CLOSE

START READING
READ

TITLE INFORMATION
INFO

PAGE PREVIEW

PAGE TURNING
BACK　NEXT

Published by AV² by Weigl
350 5ᵗʰ Avenue, 59ᵗʰ Floor New York, NY 10118
Website: www.av2books.com

Library of Congress Control Number: 2016930580

ISBN 978-1-4896-5251-5 (Hardcover)
ISBN 978-1-4896-5253-9 (Multi-user eBook)

Copyright ©2008 by Kyowon Co., Ltd.
First published in 2008 by Kyowon Co., Ltd.

Printed in the United States of America in Brainerd, Minnesota
1 2 3 4 5 6 7 8 9 0 20 19 18 17 16

032016
012916

2

Once upon a time,
there was a generous king
and a kind queen.

They did not have any children.
This made them very sad.

They wished for the fairies
to bless them with a child.

Soon after, the queen had a baby girl.

"I am very thankful," said the queen.

The king was so happy that
he threw a party.

He invited seven magical fairies
to meet his daughter.

Each fairy gave the princess
a different gift.

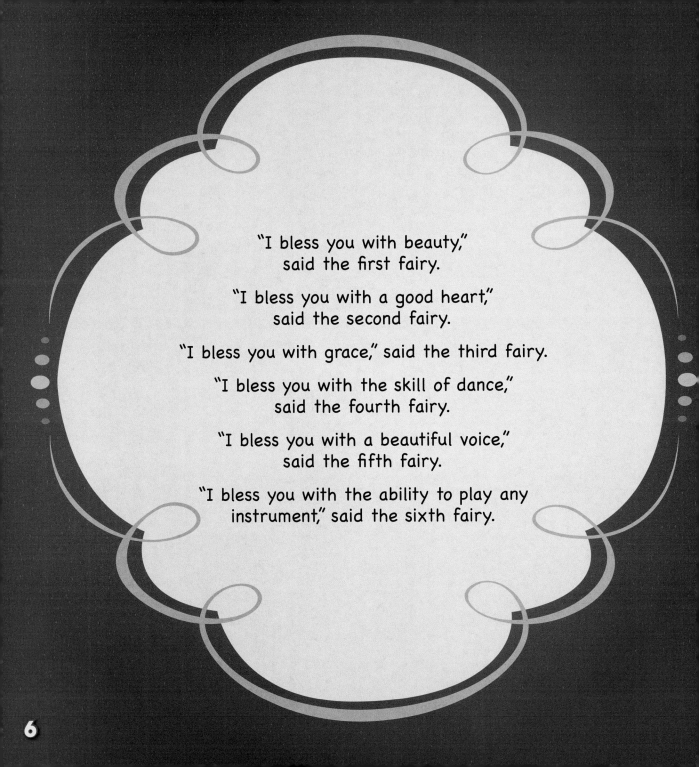

"I bless you with beauty,"
said the first fairy.

"I bless you with a good heart,"
said the second fairy.

"I bless you with grace," said the third fairy.

"I bless you with the skill of dance,"
said the fourth fairy.

"I bless you with a beautiful voice,"
said the fifth fairy.

"I bless you with the ability to play any
instrument," said the sixth fairy.

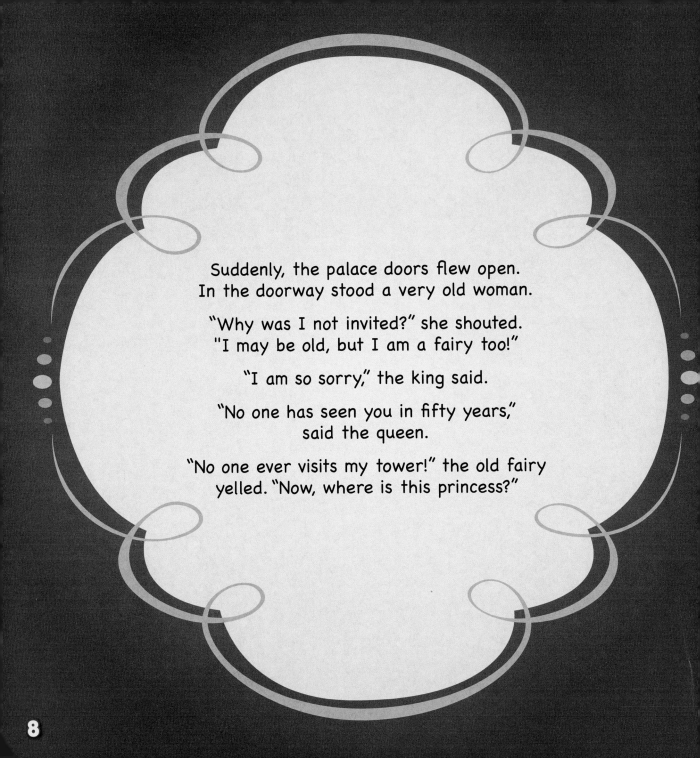

Suddenly, the palace doors flew open.
In the doorway stood a very old woman.

"Why was I not invited?" she shouted.
"I may be old, but I am a fairy too!"

"I am so sorry," the king said.

"No one has seen you in fifty years,"
said the queen.

"No one ever visits my tower!" the old fairy
yelled. "Now, where is this princess?"

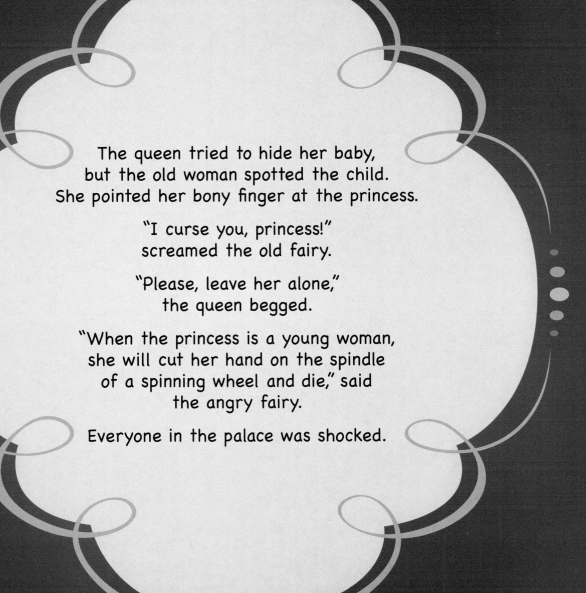

The queen tried to hide her baby,
but the old woman spotted the child.
She pointed her bony finger at the princess.

"I curse you, princess!"
screamed the old fairy.

"Please, leave her alone,"
the queen begged.

"When the princess is a young woman,
she will cut her hand on the spindle
of a spinning wheel and die," said
the angry fairy.

Everyone in the palace was shocked.

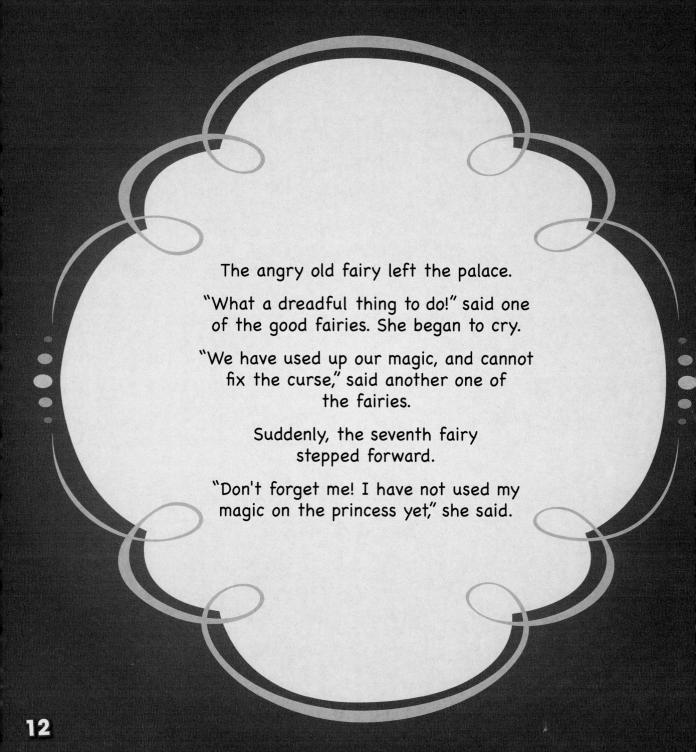

The angry old fairy left the palace.

"What a dreadful thing to do!" said one
of the good fairies. She began to cry.

"We have used up our magic, and cannot
fix the curse," said another one of
the fairies.

Suddenly, the seventh fairy
stepped forward.

"Don't forget me! I have not used my
magic on the princess yet," she said.

"Can you reverse the old fairy's curse?"
asked the queen.

"No, her magic is too powerful," said the
seventh fairy. "But I can stop the princess
from dying."

"How?" the king asked.

"If the princess is cut by the spindle
of a spinning wheel, she will not die,"
the fairy replied.

"Instead, she will fall into a deep sleep
for one hundred years," she continued.

"One day, a prince will come
to wake her."

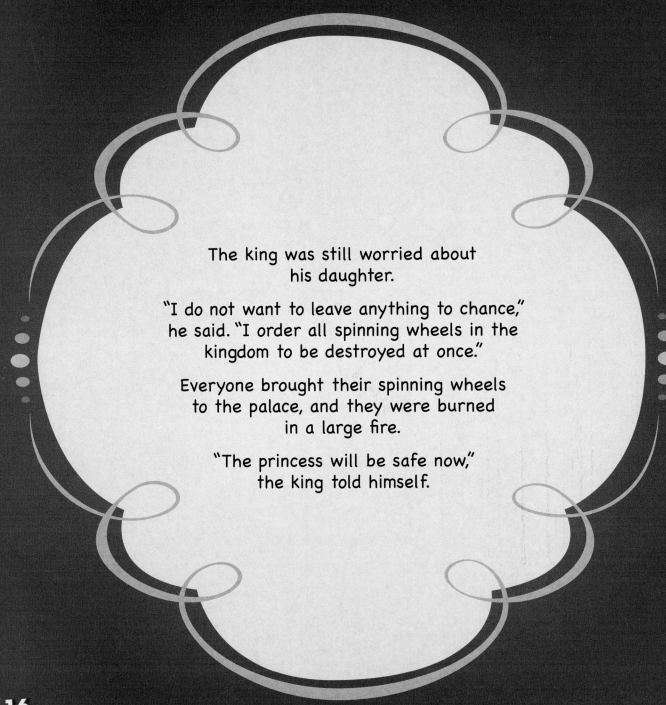

The king was still worried about
his daughter.

"I do not want to leave anything to chance,"
he said. "I order all spinning wheels in the
kingdom to be destroyed at once."

Everyone brought their spinning wheels
to the palace, and they were burned
in a large fire.

"The princess will be safe now,"
the king told himself.

Years passed, and the princess
became a young woman.

One day, she was
exploring the castle by herself.

"I wonder what is at the top of this
tower," she thought.

As she neared the top of the tower,
the princess heard a funny sound.

"What could that be?" she whispered.

When she reached the top
of the stairs, she saw a woman
using a strange wooden machine.

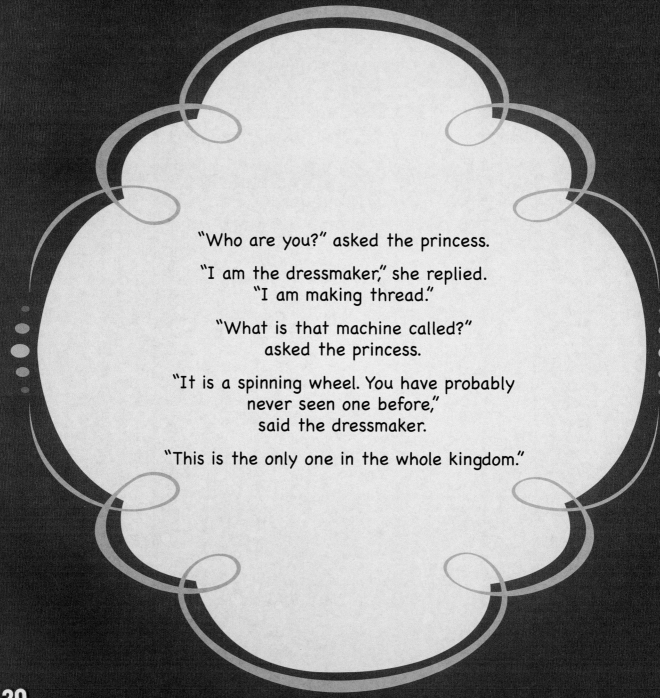

"Who are you?" asked the princess.

"I am the dressmaker," she replied.
"I am making thread."

"What is that machine called?"
asked the princess.

"It is a spinning wheel. You have probably
never seen one before,"
said the dressmaker.

"This is the only one in the whole kingdom."

"Why is this the only spinning wheel?" asked the princess.

"The king ordered them all destroyed," the dressmaker replied.

"I needed one to make clothes for the palace, so I kept this one hidden."

"How does it work?" asked the princess. "Can I try?"

The lady handed the princess the spindle, but the princess did not know how to hold it. She suddenly felt a sharp pain in her hand.

"Ouch!" she cried, falling to the floor.

"Somebody, help!" the woman yelled.

The palace guards carried the sleeping
princess to her bedroom.
It was at the top of the tallest tower.

"How could this happen?" the queen cried.

"I ordered all of the spinning wheels to be
burned," said the king.

"Will it really take one hundred years until
she wakes up?" sobbed the queen.

Just then, the seventh fairy flew in
through the open window.

"I am so sorry," the fairy said sadly.

"Is there anything you can do?"
the queen begged.

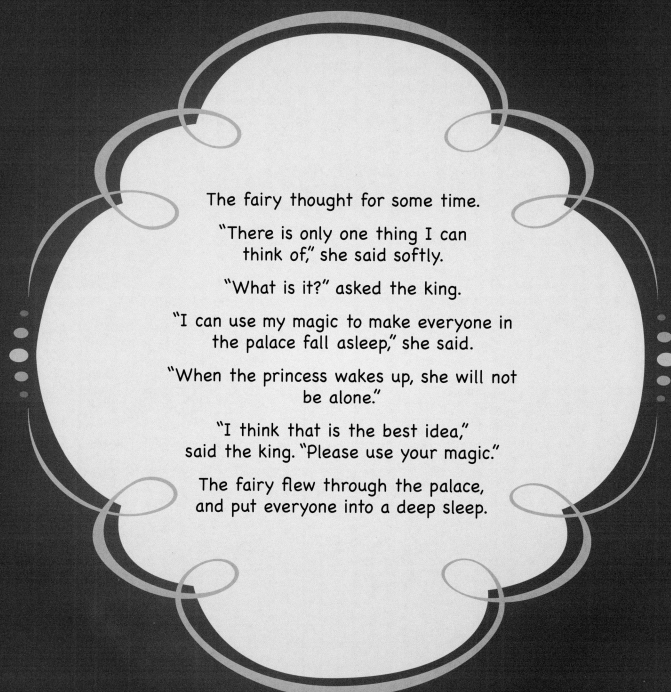

The fairy thought for some time.

"There is only one thing I can think of," she said softly.

"What is it?" asked the king.

"I can use my magic to make everyone in the palace fall asleep," she said.

"When the princess wakes up, she will not be alone."

"I think that is the best idea," said the king. "Please use your magic."

The fairy flew through the palace, and put everyone into a deep sleep.

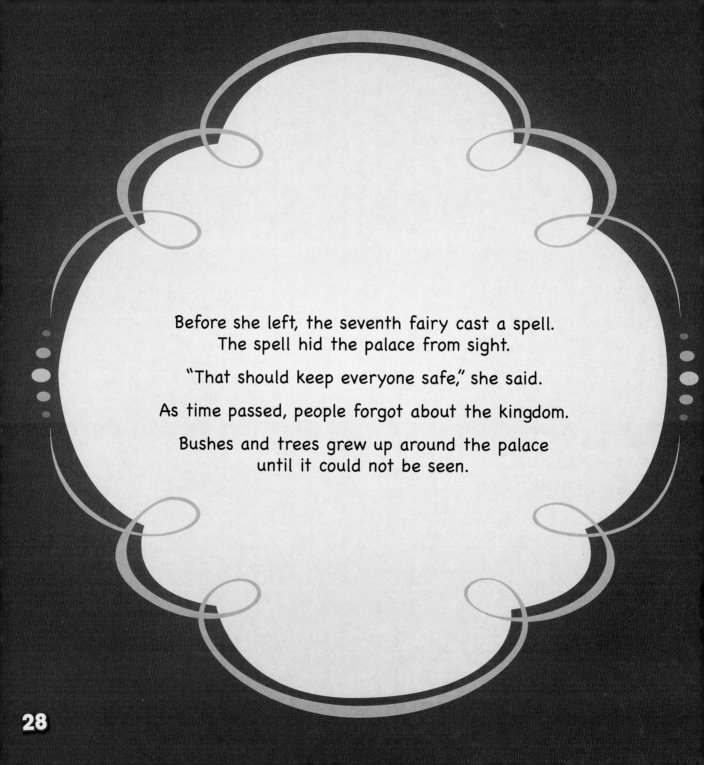

Before she left, the seventh fairy cast a spell.
The spell hid the palace from sight.

"That should keep everyone safe," she said.

As time passed, people forgot about the kingdom.

Bushes and trees grew up around the palace
until it could not be seen.

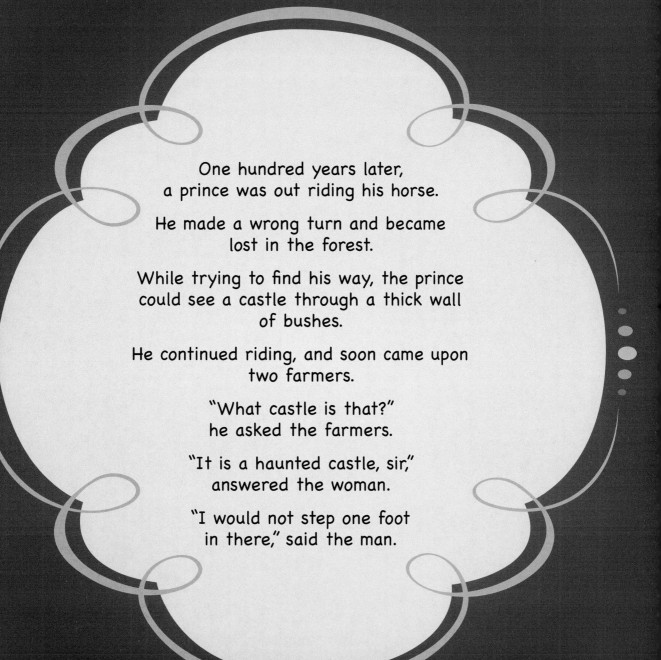

One hundred years later,
a prince was out riding his horse.

He made a wrong turn and became
lost in the forest.

While trying to find his way, the prince
could see a castle through a thick wall
of bushes.

He continued riding, and soon came upon
two farmers.

"What castle is that?"
he asked the farmers.

"It is a haunted castle, sir,"
answered the woman.

"I would not step one foot
in there," said the man.

"Why is the palace haunted?"
asked the prince.

"They say that everyone in the castle
is sleeping," replied the man.

"They have been sleeping for
one hundred years," the woman added.

"Why will they not wake up?"
the prince wondered.

"They will not wake until a prince
comes to rescue the princess,"
said the woman.

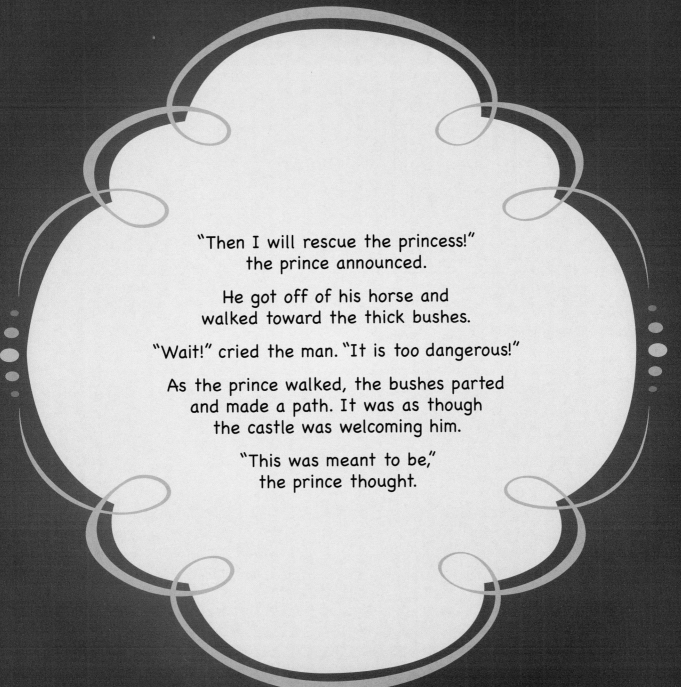

"Then I will rescue the princess!"
the prince announced.

He got off of his horse and
walked toward the thick bushes.

"Wait!" cried the man. "It is too dangerous!"

As the prince walked, the bushes parted
and made a path. It was as though
the castle was welcoming him.

"This was meant to be,"
the prince thought.

The prince walked through the palace gates.

"Oh, my!" he gasped.
"Everyone is fast asleep."

The prince walked up to a snoring guard.

"Wake up!" he demanded, shaking the guard.

The guard continued to snore,
and would not wake.

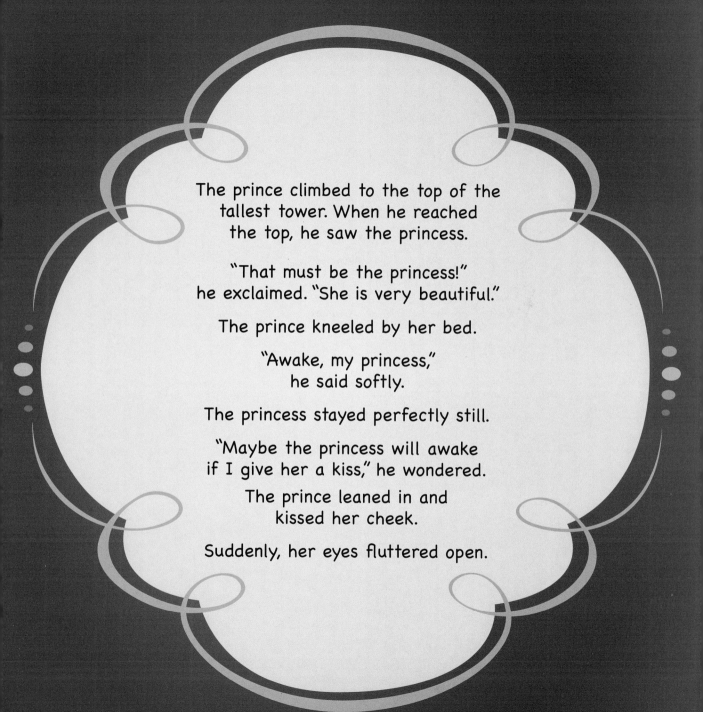

The prince climbed to the top of the
tallest tower. When he reached
the top, he saw the princess.

"That must be the princess!"
he exclaimed. "She is very beautiful."

The prince kneeled by her bed.

"Awake, my princess,"
he said softly.

The princess stayed perfectly still.

"Maybe the princess will awake
if I give her a kiss," he wondered.

The prince leaned in and
kissed her cheek.

Suddenly, her eyes fluttered open.

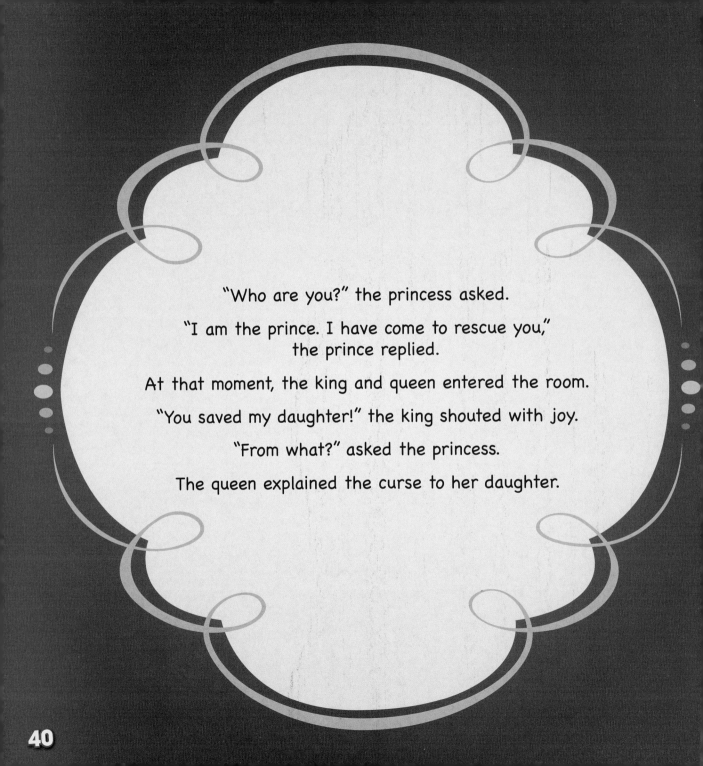

"Who are you?" the princess asked.

"I am the prince. I have come to rescue you,"
the prince replied.

At that moment, the king and queen entered the room.

"You saved my daughter!" the king shouted with joy.

"From what?" asked the princess.

The queen explained the curse to her daughter.

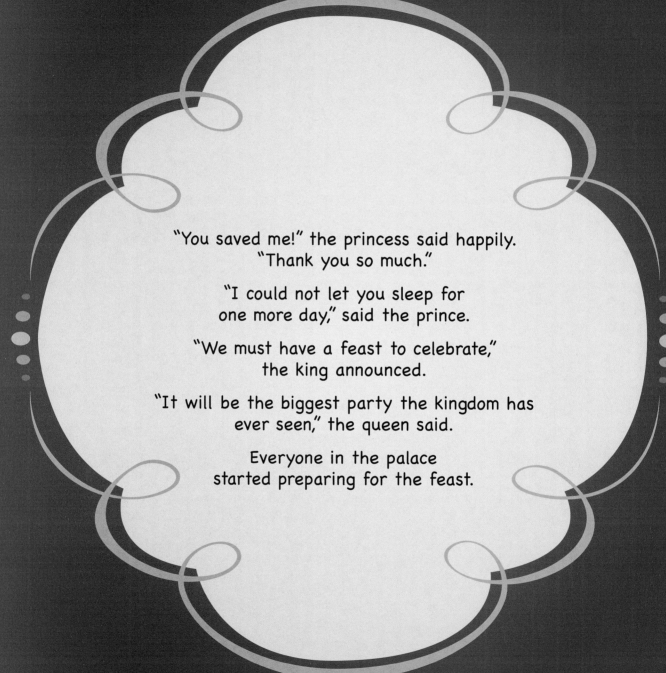

"You saved me!" the princess said happily.
"Thank you so much."

"I could not let you sleep for
one more day," said the prince.

"We must have a feast to celebrate,"
the king announced.

"It will be the biggest party the kingdom has
ever seen," the queen said.

Everyone in the palace
started preparing for the feast.

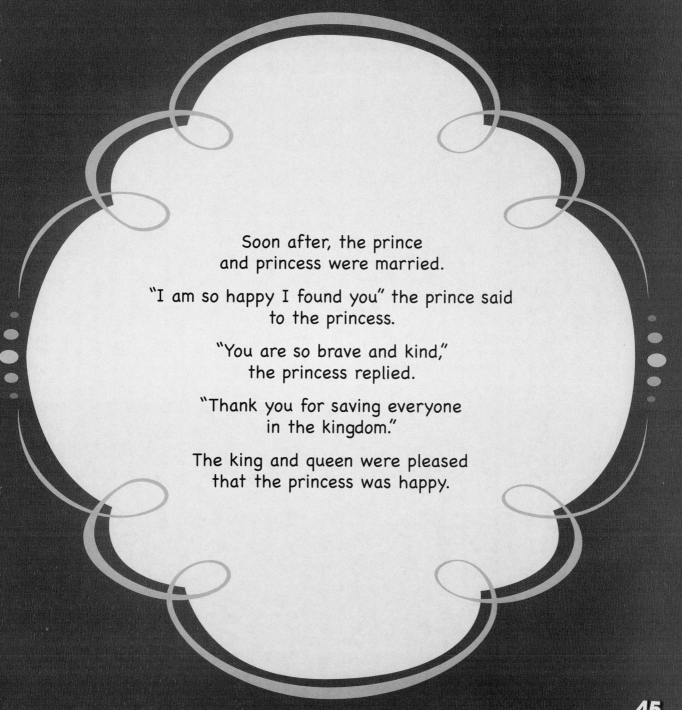

Soon after, the prince
and princess were married.

"I am so happy I found you" the prince said
to the princess.

"You are so brave and kind,"
the princess replied.

"Thank you for saving everyone
in the kingdom."

The king and queen were pleased
that the princess was happy.

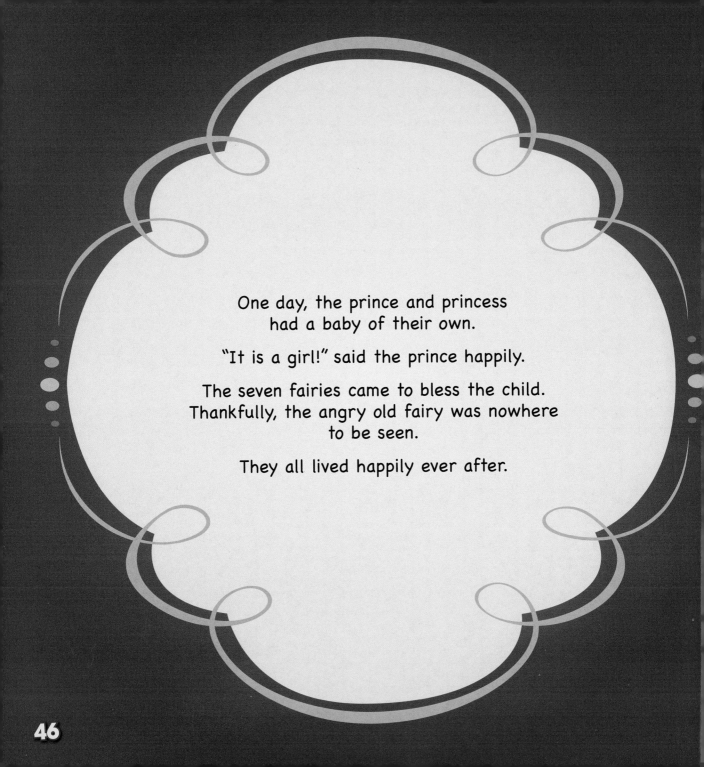

One day, the prince and princess
had a baby of their own.

"It is a girl!" said the prince happily.

The seven fairies came to bless the child.
Thankfully, the angry old fairy was nowhere
to be seen.

They all lived happily ever after.

Charles Perrault was born in 1628 in Paris, France. He studied law and worked as an administrator for the King of France. In 1695, Perrault lost his government post, and decided to write stories for children.

In 1697, Perrault published a collection of fairy tales entitled *Tales and Stories of the Past with Morals*, now known as *Tales of Mother Goose*. One of these tales was *Sleeping Beauty*. He loosely based *Sleeping Beauty* on a story published in 1634 by Giambattista Basile titled *Sun, Moon, and Talia*. Perrault's tales were very popular in France and influenced later fairy tale writers such as the Brothers Grimm.